W9-AHG-870

Sweet Dreams, Willy

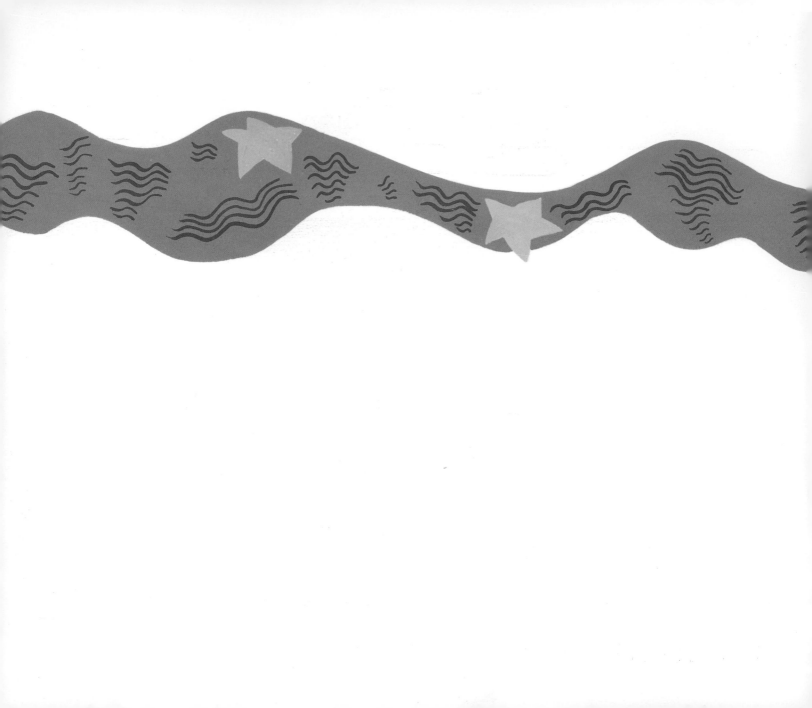

Sweet Dreams, Willy

LIZI BOYD

VIKING

For my newborn son Timothy,

the sweetest dream of all

VIKING
Published by the Penguin Group
Viking Penguin, a division of Penguin Books USA Inc.,
375 Hudson Street, New York, New York 10014, U.S.A.
Penguin Books Ltd, 27 Wrights Lane, London W8 5TZ, England
Penguin Books Australia Ltd, Ringwood, Victoria, Australia
Penguin Books Canada Ltd, 10 Alcorn Avenue, Toronto, Ontario, Canada M4V 3B2
Penguin Books (N.Z.) Ltd, 182–190 Wairau Road, Auckland 10, New Zealand

Penguin Books Ltd, Registered Offices: Harmondsworth, Middlesex, England

First published in 1992 by Viking Penguin, a division of Penguin Books USA Inc.

1   3   5   7   9   10   8   6   4   2

Copyright © Lizi Boyd, 1992
All rights reserved
Library of Congress Cataloging-in-Publication Data
Boyd, Lizi, 1953–
Sweet dreams, Willy / by Lizi Boyd.   p.   cm.
Summary: Not wanting to sleep at bedtime, Willy goes in
search of others still awake, thus beginning adventures in
a night world with birds, fish, the moon, and stars.
ISBN 0-670-84382-2 (hardcover)
[1. Night—Fiction.]   I. Title.
PZ7.B6924Sw   1992   [E]—dc20
91-28224   CIP   AC
Printed in Hong Kong
Set in Egyptian 505

Willy didn't like to go to bed. His parents
pranced and played and finally said, "Bedtime."

"Climb on," said his dad. He read Willy a book,

then turned out the light and said, "Sweet dreams."

"Somewhere, someone is still awake,"
whispered Willy as he fell asleep.

He floated up between the earth and sky, up where
dreams begin. "Hello, who is awake?" called Willy.

"I am," said a bird. "Come fly with me." They
went high above the sleeping houses.

They flew above a meadow. "Why are all the
flowers closed?" asked Willy.

"They are resting, washed in dew," said the
bird. "In the morning they will open again."

Willy and the bird flew into the forest. "Here
is my nest," said the bird. "Sweet dreams."

Willy climbed down into the black forest.

"Hello, who is awake?" called Willy.

"Join us," said the deer, "and have an apple.

You must be hungry if you're still awake."

Willy followed the deer to a fir grove. They
stood close together for warmth, ready for sleep.

"Sweet dreams," whispered the deer.

Willy wandered through the night.

"Hello, who is awake?" he called.

"I am," said a jumping fish. "Come swim with me."

Willy and the fish swam to the bottom of the pond.

All the other fish were circling their nests.

"Sweet dreams," said the watery bubbles.

Willy swam up and sat on the edge of the pond.

"Hello, who is awake?" called Willy.

"I am," said the wind. "Come sail with me."

The wind and Willy floated high in the sky.

"Now the air is still," said the wind. "It
is time for me to rest. Sweet dreams."

Willy sailed between the blues and blacks.

Willy wished he were in bed. Suddenly he was tired.

"Hello, who is awake?" called Willy.

"We are," said the stars. "Come meet the moon."

"Hello," said the moon. "Why aren't you asleep?"

"I wanted to see who was awake," said Willy, yawning.

"It is only me and the stars," said the moon.

"We make the light for your dreams and night."

"Come sit with me," said the moon, "and you
will see the night earth below."

Willy saw the sleeping houses, the birds, fish,
and animals, even the still and resting wind.

"Would someone carry me back to my bed?" asked
Willy, rubbing his sleepy eyes.

"I will," said a star. They rode through the
night sky down into Willy's cozy bed.

"Sweet dreams," said the twinkling star.

"Sweet dreams," said sleepy Willy.